Bespoke

Contents

For *my* Rocky.

Threads

BEFORE MY FINGERS COULD even grip a pair of grown-up shears properly, my dad had already instilled in me the essence of tailoring. 'Keep your shears as sharp as your reputation, Calisha,' he would say, his Trini accent drawing out the syllables over the King's English, wagging the shears in his hand as if punctuating each word.

He wanted me to take over his bespoke tailor shop; Mama wanted me to be a surgeon. She used to buy me the plastic doctor sets hanging up over the counter at the bodega. Dad got me safety scissors and thread.

The stethoscope never felt as good as the scissors, and I didn't have any siblings to examine, so guess who won that battle?

Damp spring air clung to me as I swept, the broom's rhythmic swishes anchoring me in the serene Brooklyn morning. In the distance, the commuter bus's orange lights glowed as it knelt for a woman in navy scrubs, with a thermos in her hand. Despite the early hour, I hoped my tidy storefront and credentials sign would draw in potential clients, though my unconventional role as a female tailor often bred skepticism.

The men who had bought suits from my dad, they were the hardest to win over. I hung in there, though, and eventually started detailing suits for them, their brothers, and their sons.

My daily ritual of sweeping the doorway marked my tiny rebellion against tradition's limits, proudly affirming my capabilities regardless of expectations. Dad did it every day before he opened this shop, as did my granddad before him. Granddad always told *him* it was more than just cleaning, it was respect for the store and its clients.

Sunlight streamed in as I drew back the curtains, bathing the rows of neatly arranged fabrics and tools. They were a testament to the meticulous standards ingrained in me. I adjusted a bolt of dark brocade, ensuring its perfect alignment. Each material told unique stories, some already realized through my skillful hands, others awaiting crafting by my tireless passion.

Though confident in my talents, hesitation flickered within me when facing unfamiliar clients. I feared judgement of my masculine style. Or worse, ridicule.

They didn't know what to expect from me, and I didn't blame them.

But when I tamped down uncertainty with action, their smiles came easily. The flawless execution of their visions and details hand-sewn into waistcoats spoke for themselves. My competence spoke for itself through precise cuts and impeccable stitches. Here, surrounded by my craft, I stopped having to defend my unconventionality. My work transcended gender roles. I had earned that.

One of my loyal clients' wedding suits lay before me, my canvas. Each snip and stitch channeled creativity, bringing life to dreams he had of walking his kid down the aisle. They were probably dreams he had before she was even born. I hummed along, lost in imaginative flow.

Looking up at the mirror, I smoothed the collar of my button-down shirt, and tugged at the hem of the vest, tie and sleeve garters which were my armor against skeptics. For the eagle-eyed, it was a preview of what I promised: a neat, sharp fit.

My tailored suit, a defiance of societal norms, hugged my masculine figure. It was my line in the sand. Defying every 'should' and 'ought to' about a woman's dress code.

My mother's soft, feminine form skipped me entirely. Sewing my first custom suit was easy, because I didn't have her flared hips. My vest laid nearly flat against my chest. I was wiry like Dad. I had put careful thought into each fabric and stitch of that suit, creating something that truly reflected my identity as me, Calisha.

As I affixed a rose-gold stitch to the lapel, my eyes caught on an old photo of my father and me, before the stroke that made him hand over the shop to me. Memories stirred of my former self—me, with a fresh shoulder-length silk press, plucked brows, loose sundress, and pink lip-gloss. These days, I preferred my hair with a Cesar fade close to the scalp. I threw out everything that wasn't lip balm.

I recalled the look in Dad's eyes the first day I showed up to apprentice with him dressed in slacks and a vest instead of a skirt. His smile faded ever so slightly, graying eyebrows knitting together. He said nothing, simply gesturing for me to grab a broom. I swept until my doubts and his wordless disapproval felt further away than the scattered dust.

But dwelling on the past? Not my style. Snip—the thread cut clean, like my resolve. Keep moving forward.

Footsteps at the door snapped me back. I tucked away lingering doubts and turned with a steady smile to greet Mr. Jenkins. "We have a grandbaby yet?"

His dismissive wave couldn't hide the growing smile. That baby was going to be spoiled rotten whenever he decided to make his grand appearance. "Oh, he's still being stubborn."

"Little dude is all comfy, but he'll come out when he's ready." I retrieved his suit from the box for him to take to the back and try on. "Try that on, see how it feels. I gave the collar a little more slack for you."

When he emerged from behind the curtain, his shoulders filled out the tailored suit beautifully. The fit was impeccable, accentuating his big and tall stature without compromising his comfort. His smile beamed with satisfaction as he surveyed himself in the mirror. Men often looked into that mirror and found their true selves revealed through their suits.

"You've truly outdone yourself." He smoothed down the collar of his jacket with genuine appreciation. "I feel like a new man in this suit. And you were right about the button detail. You've never steered me wrong."

I beamed. "I'm not happy until you're happy."

"I am. Hey, Cal. My niece, Rockeisha, needs a tuxedo for a wedding. Would you mind if I referred her here?"

"I'd be honored, Mr. Jenkins. Truly."

Hm. I had never designed a pantsuit for another woman before. We'd served women, of course, but they were rare. Mostly they preferred to buy dress suits from department stores. But helping a woman look good in a tuxedo? Should be an interesting challenge.

A challenge I was up for.

Just Extra Enough

THE SHOP'S DOORBELL RINGING snapped me clean out of the steady rhythm of pinning fabric. New customer? Someone selling DVDs? As I looked up, a silhouette framed in the late-afternoon sunlight greeted me. Long brown dreadlocks draped over a crisp cream-colored track suit with white lines down the sides, which popped vibrant against her smooth, dark skin. A woman stepped in, her youthful, athletic frame a stark contrast to the aging gentlemen who shuffled into my shop.

The way she scanned the shop, a hint of curiosity and delight in her eyes, suggested she wasn't a stranger to places like these. Yet, there was something tentative in her step, as if each visit still held a new discovery.

This sudden break in my day's monotony made me stand up straight. Clearly, this woman enjoyed looking good.

She was in the right place.

"Hello! Welcome to Duke's Tailor Shop," I called out.

"You're Cal, right?" The woman's smile, revealing a dimple at her chin, made me want to bite my bottom lip. Her voice was a mix of melody and confidence. "Rocky. Heard all about you from Uncle Charles."

"Ah, Mr. Jenkins, right? He's been a client for years." I shook her hand as I nodded in recognition. This must be the Rockeisha he kept going on about, puffing out his chest with pride. If I recalled correctly, she was a physician's assistant for the local hospital.

Her firm grip lingered in a reassuring way.

"Nice to meet you, Cal." Her broad smile suggested a charismatic air. She quickly looked me up and down, before averting her eyes. "Got a wedding on the horizon. The bride's put me on a no off-the-rack list. Kind of like a no-fly list." Her chuckle was low and rich, velvet over gravel. "Guess it's time for the big leagues, huh?"

We had long breezed past the suit's occasion, which was the most important question when facing a potential client. You wouldn't suggest a tuxedo out of the gate for the guy who just wants to impress his boss enough to get the raise, right?

"Sounds like a close friend," I ventured, my curiosity piqued.

Rocky smirked. "Something like that."

I ushered Rocky towards the consultation area, eager to focus on the task at hand. We walked past rows of garment spools. A bust of a plaid gray suit with a vest donned with an electric blue handkerchief that spilled from the pocket. "Let's discuss colors and styles. What type of venue is the wedding?"

"An upscale vineyard," she answered, showing me a picture on her phone of the swanky location. The lush green rows of vines stretched out behind an elegant gazebo at golden hour, setting the stage for a sophisticated event.

"Beautiful," I said, my mind already envisioning the perfect suit. Or, rather, her in it. I twisted my attention to the row of jacket busts, each displaying a different style of jacket. Single-breasted, double-breasted, Neapolitan jacket shouldered, pinstriped with gold stitches.

We explored options that would suit her frame. Considering the wedding setting, I suggested incorporating a provision for a flower in the lapel. Rocky seemed pleased with the idea.

She paused before a bust of a floral tuxedo jacket, her gaze lingering with an appreciation that seemed more personal than casual. "This looks like a dress Mom used to have. Hey, do you think a pattern would be doing the absolute most?"

"No, not for a wedding, for a nice pop of flair. Have you considered any particular colors?" I grinned, watching as Rocky gave the bust a full 360 view. She was wearing some citrus-smelling cologne, crisp and masculine. If I were a cartoon, I would have floated.

The way she studied the jacket, eyes drinking in the details, I couldn't help but to drink *her* in. Her casual designer style formed a striking contrast to the elegant pieces before her. I admired how her locs were pinned back neatly in rows, highlighting flawless brown skin. Her feet were clad in the same boldly colorful high-end sneakers I had coveted but wouldn't splurge on. As I pictured refined tailoring accentuating her athletic build, I understood her wonder—outward presentation not only reflected the inner self but revealed fresh depths.

We talked about jacket styles and lapels, and when she pointed to a specific tuxedo jacket, excitement passed through me. Seldom did I get to tailor for masculine women like myself.

"Something like this?" She pointed towards a photo of a stud model wearing a sleek patterned tuxedo jacket, fingers pulling up the lapel of the tuxedo, as if the model was adjusting herself in front of a mirror.

"I think that'll work for the formality of the event, sure. This collar would be stunning with a floral or damask pattern, if you're interested." I pointed towards an angled shawl-collar.

"Something in the burgundy family, yeah," she mused, glancing over at me. "The theme colors are burgundy and peach. Fall wedding."

"Both great choices." I nodded, my mind working overtime to envision the perfect suit to complement her figure and style. Her shoulder width looked like it could support a roll crown on the sleeve, which would give the suit I pictured for her more structure and elegance. It would taper gracefully into a smaller waist.

She edged closer. "Just the right amount of *extra*, you think?"

"If you can't go extra at a wedding, when can you, right? Here are some fabric options for your suit lining." I presented Rocky a sample book. "Take your time and let me know which one speaks to you."

She flipped through the patterns, stopping on a deep burgundy damask sample. Her eyes lit up as she ran a finger over the pattern. "This one right here is casket sharp." Straight white teeth sat in a cradle of moisturized, succulent lips, with that dimpled chin. It had my stomach fluttering as she made her choices.

My throat dried up. "It's, uh, beautiful." A thrill at her excitement made me pull at the measure tape hanging around my neck. Words didn't matter. They tumbled out all wrong, like a toddler learning how to talk. "It will make a—make a statement."

"Great! Let's go with this," she decided, handing me back the swatch. Our fingers accidentally brushed with the movement, and I turned away to keep her from seeing my face burn hot at the touch.

"Alright, I'll need to schedule an appointment to take measurements." I forced myself to focus. "How does Tuesday at 3 PM work for you?"

"Perfect!" she beamed. "I can't wait to see how everything comes together."

"Me neither," I admitted, surprised by the sincerity in my voice. I took Rocky's deposit for the suit order and handed her a receipt. The card was a promise of more time spent in her company.

"Thank you, Cal." Rocky tucked the receipt into her wallet. "I really appreciate your help with this. I feel like I'm in good hands."

"Of course," I tried to hang onto my composure, thankful there was no one there to point out how I leaned over the counter. "It's my pleasure, Rocky."

Whew, boy. She just didn't know how *much*. Being so close to her made me want to melt on the spot under the warmth of her smile. Wait, what? Was this a *crush*? How?!

I scheduled our first appointment, cursing my fluttering heart. Rocky's magnetic pull was undeniable, but I reminded myself to stay professional. This was about crafting the perfect pantsuit, not getting into *her* pantsuit.

We exchanged goodbyes as she headed towards the door; the chimes jingled once more as she stepped out into the warm sunlight. The shop seemed to grow dimmer without her presence.

I busied myself tidying the consultation area, willing my hands to be still as I neatly refolded fabric swatches and lined up pencils and pens with excess care. I swept up imaginary specks of dust, shook out the tailor's tape as if new creases might manifest. I wiped the consultation table for the third time, banishing any slow-motion visuals before they took root. Anything to divert this restless energy that kept drawing my eyes to the tablet's appointment app, still open on the counter.

There was no reason one client should've unraveled my calm so effortlessly.

The consultation had flown by in a blur of fabric swatches, enthusiastic gestures, and Rocky's dimpled, megawatt smile. Emphasis on that last part.

This was so unlike me—I didn't mix business with pleasure. Yet there was something captivating about her that tugged at me. Probably had some smitten older woman slipping her extra oxtail at the Jamaican spot up the street, with extra gravy. And stayed besties with all her exes, too.

I chided myself for concocting stories about a stranger just because I found her attractive. But I would see her again soon, and that meant I might get to know her. The thought alone made restless hands fidget for new things to tinker with.

Closing up shop for the evening, I failed to tamp down the half-smile she had coaxed from me against all my resolve.

Hey, Big Head

THE INTRICATE SUIT JACKET embroidery was just starting to take shape under my fingers. I snipped the last bit of thread off the cuff, testing the tug of the button. Just enough slack.

The door bell rang, and I tucked my chin to keep my face from giving away even a hint of a goofy grin. "Cal!" came Rocky's enthused voice, and the corners of my mouth lifted in defiance of my wishes.

My face fell slightly when I saw that she was here with a beautiful woman who had flawless cafe-au-lait skin. She was shorter than Rocky, and her thick thighs accentuated her flattering pear shape. A teal sundress hugged her soft figure and her stylish ginger bob swayed as she followed Rocky into the shop.

We had a third wheel. Better make nice.

"Hey, how's it going?" I greeted them both with a wide smile as fake as Nylon.

"What's up?" Rocky grinned, her eyes sparkling. "We have a guest." She gestured towards the shorter woman next to her.

"I'm just here to make sure she doesn't pick out any wild patterns or anything." The woman gave Rocky side eye as she nudged her with her hip.

"Nice to meet you." I shook the woman's hand firmly to mask my unease. Though unplaced, an unexpected twinge of jealousy stirred in me. But I tempered my grip to project a professional confidence I didn't quite feel. Well, there's that. My dreams dashed, finally. *Good.* I turned back to Rocky. "So, when are the two of you walking down the aisle?"

Rocky let out a surprised laugh. "Big Head. When you getting married again?"

The woman rolled her eyes. "Your mama's a big head."

"And you have her forehead," Rocky teased. "Cal, meet my cousin, Big Head. She's the bride."

She waved. "I'm *Jayla*, nice to meet you."

Oh, boy. I cleared my throat, grasping for composure. "Shall we get started on the fitting then?" I busied myself prepping the pieces, avoiding eye contact.

As Rocky disappeared behind the barrier to change into a more fitted shirt, I couldn't resist watching her silhouette. Jayla and Rocky continued to crack jokes on each other. They reminded me of my mom when she was with her siblings. She emerged with a white tank, showing off arms that looked sculpted in the gym. The dip of stomach between her shirt and her pants dried my throat up.

Her left arm had the beginnings of a tattoo sleeve, stopping mid bicep.

"Ready for some adjustments?" I willed my voice to sound casual. Under the pretense of pinning for the perfect fit, I relished gently guiding Rocky's toned limbs. My hands trembled slightly, but I managed to hide it by tugging on the measuring tape. I waved them both over the staging area and directed Rocky to the podium.

"Face forward for me," I said, barely a whisper. "Let's see what we have here."

This close to Rocky, I could smell that cologne again, the same citrus scent she wore to the consultation.

Remembering the scent a person's wearing. That was the first sign of doom, wasn't it?

I pulled the measuring tape from around my neck, brain already kicking into gear. "I'm going to measure your chest size, if that's okay? I'll need to step into your space a little, but I'll try to be quick."

"Not a problem." Rocky's dark eyes met mine with a direct smile I could only describe as reassuring.

I didn't want to mess up this first appointment by being a creeper or anything.

"Right, of course," I looked away. I worked on auto-pilot until the alluring scent of Rocky's cologne hit me again when I stepped close to wrap the measuring tape around her bust. But not too close.

Trying to hide the inner turmoil, I cleared my throat and spoke with forced calm. This time, I made myself look her in the eyes. "I apologize for invading your personal space. It's just necessary to get an accurate measurement."

Rocky's eyes sparkled with understanding, and her voice bounced with mischief. "You can come closer, if you need to. If it'll help."

Jayla cleared her throat. For both of us. I froze.

"Everything alright?" Rocky asked, her eyebrow raised in concern as she noticed my hesitation.

"Of course," I assured her with a forced smile. My heart raced at her closeness. Could she sense it? There was something about this woman that jumpstarted me alive. Senses on fire, alert. She terrified me at the same time. I tried to shake off those thoughts as I focused on the job at hand, but they lingered, like an itch I couldn't quite reach.

"You're going to be a thirty-four." I jotted the number on my pad to record the bust size. I grabbed a dark blue blazer from the back and directed her to put it on. The movement of her body made her heady scent float past my nostrils again. Damn. This was torture.

I tried to maneuver around Rocky, allowing her a sense of comfort and space as I took measurements of her chest, sleeves, armpits, biceps and shoulders, sliding the ruler tape's length down to the cuff. With each measurement, I grew more frustrated by my body's own involuntary reaction to Rocky's closeness. My pulse quickened. Hers answered mine. Her pulse startled under my touch. As I worked, my head became dizzy, stomach feeling like I'd held a breath too long and let it out too quickly.

The sleeve cuff measurement recorded, my hands hesitated at her waist. I noted the way she sucked in a breath when the cool tape touched the bare space between her shirt and her pants.

"I'll need to measure your waist next." My smile was lightning quick. I slipped my fingers in between her stomach and her pants, ensuring no more than a finger's width in between the pants and her skin. My fingers connected with the heated skin above her boxers. Rocky was a boxer briefs person. My belly flipped with nerves, and if I could have yanked my fingers back, I would have. "Just, uh, making sure that we leave no more than half an inch between the suit and your stomach. You're twenty-four inches."

Rocky swallowed hard. Her eyes darkened when they met mine. "Uh. Hm. Yeah."

Next, God forgive me, I needed to measure her hips and thighs, her inseam. She had a thirty-five inch hip. Practically an hourglass shape, even as muscular as she was. Hips as flared as hers would present a challenge, keeping the eye in balance with the rest of the suit. Muscular thighs needed to be in proportion with the pant. 'Tapered fit,' I scribbled.

Out of my periphery, Rocky's stare lingered on me as I wrote. Her eyes tracked the motions like my mundane tailor tasks were riveting choreography. I dared a glance upward. When our gazes met, a breathless vice-grip tension seized the room. The wanting in Rocky's expression snatched mine right up to mirror it—naked, vulnerable.

I broke the gaze first, feeling suddenly out of my depth. I peeked around Rocky to look at Jayla. The way her neck snapped to her phone was a bit too sudden. Her eyebrows had somehow crawled up to her hairline, almost.

My hands might have granted me a few moments of surety in my measurements, but in that moment, they felt unsteady. This wasn't like me, this wavering. But there it was, undeniable and confusing as all hell.

I had suddenly questioned my own wisdom, taking her on as a client knowing I had to do this fitting. Knowing I had to take up her space, breathe her air, feel her body so close to mine.

I absolutely, truly hated myself.

As I reached for the measuring tape, it slipped from my fingers, unraveling across the floor, a mirror of my own unraveling composure. I was a fraud; the facade of poise cracked wide open, literally at her feet.

"Allow me," Rocky offered with a hint of gallantry, but I was quicker, retrieving the tape before the offer turned into action.

"Don't move. Thanks, no, I've got it—" I stood to regain control of the situation. I measured Rocky's thigh again, which took longer due to my arousal and her closeness. Sweat beaded at my brow as I warred with my concentration.

"Twenty-three inches," I said, almost to myself. Wrote that down on the sheet.

I soldiered on, determined to finish before I embarrassed the both of us by doing something incredibly stupid and unprofessional. Like kissing her.

I slid the tape between hands. "I'm just going to measure your collar size, next."

"Feel free to come as close as you need to," Rocky joked. I think. *Was* that a joke? I blinked hard to steady a sudden vertigo. I willed the blood not to rush too obscenely to my cheeks and expose just how undone I was.

"Uh. Sure," I stammered, eyes darting to hers again. It was like being pinned with nowhere to move. The chemistry between us was palpable, a current whipping through the air. As our gazes locked, I wondered what she was thinking.

I didn't dare ask.

I finished the rest of the measurements in relative silence, recording each in bird scrawl.

"And we are all done."

"Each measurement needs to be perfect for the best fit." Rocky raised an eyebrow, her voice low, teasing. "Are you sure you don't need to check any of them again?"

The back of my neck flushed. "Of—of course precision is key. Can never be too thorough." I leaned in as if double-checking the tape, my eyes daring to flick up from her collarbone to meet her knowing gaze. Rocky bit her lip in response, the table-turned provocation sending nearly delirious sparks down my limbs. I was painfully, desperately aware of how little space lingered between us, gulping as my nipples puckered under my shirt. Jesus.

My brain surged into overdrive, and for the first time, I wondered if Rocky was aware of my crush and teasing me, or if maybe the attraction I felt towards her could be mutual. Was it even possible for two studs to be attracted to each other? Years of societal norms had taught me otherwise, but in that moment, with Rocky's eyes on mine, something deep in me whispered that maybe, just maybe, yeah, it was.

I'd dated femmes before. I slowed down when they entered doors, hid my disappointment when they never tried to slide hands in between my legs, and they never thought to tell me I looked beautiful too. I never got the same energy I put out. The same orgasms I gave. Things never lasted very long, and I was tired of searching for a perfect fit. I gave up.

There was no need to wonder how or *if* things would be different with a stud. Studs went with femmes; they didn't date other studs. And I wasn't going to date my client.

"We good?" Her eyes twinkled with something, the twist of her mouth teasing.

"Uh, yeah, I think—I think we're good." Snapped back to the moment, I gave her a quick smile. All business.

"Great!" Rocky's smile was warm and genuine. "I can't wait to see how the suit turns out."

"I'll get right to work on that." My heart galloped as I watched her slip off the jacket. I allowed myself to breathe deeply, freely. Licked bone-ash dry lips with relief. I had survived.

Rocky dipped into the back to change shirts again.

Jayla, who had been silent throughout our interaction, now stood off to the side. Her smile almost seemed to be hiding something as she watched us. I glanced at her, momentarily distracted from my internal chaos, and wondered if she just saw me turn into a pathetic, babbling puddle at her cousin's feet.

"Alright." Rocky walked back into the staging area. Her voice was thicker than cold porridge. She cleared her throat. "I guess we're all done here for today. Thanks, Cal." She shot me a meaningful look that sent another thrill through my veins. "I'll be back soon for my next appointment. Solo, this time."

"Of course," I tried to sound casual even though my heart raced. My voice cracked like a boy going through puberty instead. "Looking forward to it."

Please tell me I didn't say that out loud.

Oh God, I did. *Fuck*.

Jayla smirked. "You sure y'all two don't need a chaperone next fitting? I can clear my schedule if you need. Just say the word."

My cheeks burned as Rocky let out an embarrassed laugh. She soft-punched her in the arm. "Big Head, you crazy." She shook her head, avoiding my gaze. I busied myself organizing fabric samples, willing the awkward moment to pass. Still, Jayla's joke hung heavy in the room.

As they left the shop together, an odd sense of relief mixed with my disappointment. The prospect of seeing Rocky again excited me, but the nagging voice in the back of my mind told me that women like her preferred more feminine partners. I was driving myself nuts for nothing.

Shaking my head, I threw myself into the template for Rocky's suit to distract myself from my thoughts. My hands moved mechanically, but they were useless. Distracted. I erased more lines than I drew.

Eventually, I tossed the paper, done trying to salvage what I had. I couldn't shake the feeling that there was something else here, more than just a tailor-client relationship. That moment when our eyes met, the electricity that seemed to crackle in the air, the way she teased me—it felt too real to ignore.

Still, as the day wore on, my thoughts wouldn't allow me one second of peace. They would nag a hole right through my stomach if I let them eat away at the butterflies forming there. And, I would. I had a reputation to uphold. Even one careless fling with a client that reached the wrong ears would unravel that.

I didn't want Dad looking through me with disappointment yet again.

It was foolish to think she could ever see me as anything other than the weird, gangly tailor who made her suit. My face would be long forgotten as she made eyes at some pretty, stacked bridesmaid in her form-fitting burgundy dress, flirting with her all night.

Deflated, I turned my attention back to the task at hand. Dislodging these feelings was at the top of the list, next, starting the patterns on this jacket.

Crazy-making as they were, these feelings would pass.

They always did.

Paper Thin

I SAT AT MY drafting board, measuring out the patterns for Rocky's tux. The paper rasped with the glide of the ruler over it, marking out lines and curves, extra emphasis on the darts. I had one week until her next fitting, and I couldn't afford to fall further behind.

This morning, I'd posted photos of myself modeling my suits, hoping to attract more masculine, dapper women. Rocky being referred to my shop was lucky, but this was an untapped audience that I could try to reach to make my *own* clients. Not ones I inherited from my dad, but mine alone. I got an enthusiastic response from one named Dane. A little too enthusiastic for my comfort.

I glanced at another incoming message on my phone, a flirtatious note from Dane, who seemed determined to push the boundaries from professional to personal. With lips pressed together in annoyance, I lined up the metal weight on the drafting paper. These distractions could wait; precision was paramount now.

Dane, seeking more than just a tailor, would have to understand my boundaries. I'd make it clear—my shop was a place for crafting suits, not for hookups.

Maybe *I* needed reminding of that, most of all.

Returning my attention to the pattern, I focused on drawing smooth lines. The fresh smell of linen and drawing paper grounded me. Rocky, and the perfect fit of her tux demanded my full concentration.

The pencil slid smoothly down the drafting paper, tracing the length of the sleeve. I'd spend hours cutting each template if I needed to. This tux had to be flawless.

My mind drifted to Rocky herself. We hadn't discussed her dating history, or anything beyond numbers, fabrics and buttons. Had she even *been* with a stud before? The thought left me feeling as sleazy as an oil slick. I shook my head, banishing the intrusive questions. Just needed to concentrate on my craft.

I traced the smooth slope of collar to the edge of the shoulder, admiring my handiwork. If only pursuing Rocky could be so simple. Just two studs, no controversy, no ridicule, no gossip. None at all, not from my father's loyal customers, or the women I hoped to turn into clients.

Just three generations of my family business on the line, no pressure *at all.*

For now, restraint was safer, however painful. I etched a dart harder into the paper, gritting my teeth.

I transformed the blank drafting paper into a symphony of lines and curves, fashioning Rocky's dream tuxedo one measurement at a time. I was getting back into my zone.

My phone chimed with another message from Dane. I tensed, glancing over at it. She was insisting we keep things secret, claiming it was "gay" for two studs to date each other.

Dane was so eager, it didn't occur to her that at that point, she was talking to herself.

If my eyes weren't tethered to my sockets, they would have rolled clear to the back of my skull. Being forced back into the closet felt too familiar, too raw. I remember telling my dad I had a girlfriend. The way he swallowed real hard and wouldn't look at me afterward. I had never seen him more interested in a football game. The same person who once said he didn't consider American football a real sport was suddenly heavily invested in the game.

There had been subsequent conversations with my dad, but he would always steer the topic away from anything related to me or who I was dating.

"Calisha, maybe focus on the business," he had muttered. A subtle nudge to bury my personal life, as if we could fold away my identity like the unsold suits hanging in the back. Forgotten.

His discomfort wasn't loud or aggressive; it was in his prolonged silences, the way he meticulously sorted tools whenever I mentioned a date. Mama would just tighten her lips, a quiet alliance with unspoken rules, all the while the tension pulled tighter than a stubborn zipper.

I put down my tools, slid away from the desk to frown at my phone.

Dane's proposition left a bitter taste in my mouth. That cat was out of the bag; I couldn't hide my sexuality any more than I could a broken leg. Every part of me: my hair, my stride, the drape of my clothes, it was like a neon sign. Stand me next to any femme, and assumptions fly.

My thumb hovered over the block button on her profile. Then, decisively, I tapped it.

Good riddance. I slid my phone back into my desk drawer, burying it from sight.

With renewed focus, I turned back to the drafting board, scribbling scaled measurements in the chest area of the paper for the seamstress.

The pattern pieces lying mismatched on the table were like my unsorted thoughts about Rocky, waiting to be pieced together. Patterns were comforting and predictable, unlike this thing I felt. I could trust clear and steady hands to cut clean lines without hesitation. If only the rest of me was as certain.

With the last line of the sketch complete, I took a second to study my handiwork, square eraser at the ready to correct any wayward lines.

The patterns were coming along beautifully, and Rocky would look stunning in them.

I nodded in satisfaction as I held up the pattern that would become Rocky's tuxedo jacket, admiring my careful drawing. The darts were precise, and would allow just enough give in the natural folds without looking baggy, or worse, like a ready-made garment.

A nervous flutter sank in my chest and settled into my belly. Each line in the pattern was like an unanswered question.

Did she think like Dane, that something like that was best done out of sight? Or did labels not matter to her?

A pencil rolled down my desk, and my hand shot out to catch it. Thankfully, this pivoted my attention back to my task.

I snipped at a stray curl of paper outside the outline, then held up the sheet up again. Perfect. This was my realm—my craft. Here, I was in control.

I arranged the patterns, then carefully slid them into their envelope, ready to sew them into something that remotely looked like a suit.

As my fingers traced over the shawl lapel, visualizing how it would fall on Rocky's neck, how it would slope down to broad shoulders. Crisp, yet effortlessly elegant.

My own shoulders tensed as I pushed the thought away.

As an openly gay woman running my dad's business, it was hard enough. Some people weren't as progressive as they claimed to be. I didn't want to be the topic of Sunday's dinner, with my private life up for consumption the same way my dad saw others.

Suppressing my desires was the wiser choice, even if it left an ache inside me.

Outside, the street was settling into the evening. Buses let people off work. I heard the clank of metal barricades signaling the close of nearby storefronts. The faint murmur of the city beyond the shop's walls seeped through the glass, a distant reminder of the world moving on as I lost myself in my work.

Shadows stretched across the room, playing over rows of fabric bolts stacked neatly against the wall, casting the patterns in deep yellow and orange. Sunset colors. Which meant it was time to wrap it up.

With a tired huff, I slid the tape measure off my neck and started winding down for the evening. Maybe the only thing I was in the mood for was takeout, alone in my little apartment above the store, and nothing more. Me and my TV wife, Captain Olivia Benson, forever. Even if she kept making heart eyes at Elliot sometimes.

I could only hope that seeing Rocky walk out of the shop for the last time with a garment box would snuff out this crush, like a cigarette meeting the heel end of a boot.

Cuff It

THE SILVER SHEEN OF a cufflink caught the light as I adjusted the jacket's position on the mannequin, ensuring that it lay equidistant from its neighbor. My fingers skimmed over the display case glass, wiping away imaginary smudges, while folded blazers stacked on the shelves formed a backdrop of meticulous lines and creases. The spools of fabric rested in their designated spots; hues of charcoal, navy, and burgundy stood at attention like soldiers in formation. I paused, allowing my fingers to trace the spine of a fabric sample book before snapping it open to realign a slip of silk that had dared to shift out of place.

Anything to keep myself busy to distract them for the fact that I was waiting.

Focus, Cal.

My ears strained for the familiar chime of the door, heralding her arrival. Each tick of the clock was a metronome to my racing heart, counting down minutes until professionalism would have to armor me once more. Last time, our laughter had filled the room too easily, her smile igniting something that I couldn't douse with mere pleasantries.

Then, the bell above the door shattered the silence. My hands froze mid-fold as she strode in, the air shifting to accommodate her presence. Rocky was all boxy angles today in her navy blue scrubs.

"Sorry about the outfit change." Her voice was as smooth as fine silk. "Came straight from work."

"Of course, no problem at all." My voice threatened to betray the sudden jump in my pulse. Her usual casual style was absent, but the way the scrubs showed off her lean, muscular form was just unfair. I smoothed down my apron—a shield of professionalism—as if it could hide the warmth creeping onto my cheeks or the sensation in my belly.

"Let's get started then." I hoped my smile didn't reach my eyes. "You know the way by now."

"That I do." Her stride toward the dressing area was as self-assured as always.

I turned back to the accessories, giving them one last unnecessary pat. The crisp sound of fabric against fabric as she changed was a rhythmic reminder of what I needed to do. In the mirror's reflection, the studio seemed smaller somehow, the space between us charged with unspoken words and glances held a moment too long.

In those fleeting moments alone, flashes of our last encounter danced behind my eyes—a brush of hands, an accidental caress. A flush of heat raced up my neck, and I fought to extinguish it with calculations, of seams and stitches and notes.

"Ready when you are," Rocky called out, her voice pulling me back from the edge.

"Great, let's see how it fits." Anxious hands reached for the tape measure, a hard swallow steadying my resolve. I scanned the suit briefly at the white threads, the white hand-sewn stitches holding together slices of fabric to map out the beginnings of a tuxedo. I kept a piece of the paper template affixed to the cuff of the jacket with her measurements scrawled. The satin shawl lapel was an elegant slope cascading down the garment. I hope she'd be happy with that choice.

My gaze would *not* drift from the suit she wore to admire the curve of her jaw. I wouldn't let it. I swallowed impatience as her button-down shirt, left open at the neck, exposed the alluring curve of collarbone. Had to force my eyes away.

Today, I was just the tailor, and she was just the client. That was the line we wouldn't cross. Not again.

New rule: no more clients I was attracted to. Might as well jab a needle past the thimble into my thumb, over and over again. Probably didn't sting as much.

As Rocky ascended the pedestal, every eye movement, every breath seemed amplified. I began my circuit around her, hovering just above the fabric, my mind attempting to focus on the fall of the lapels, the drape of the material.

"Looks like we need some adjustments here." My voice was all business as I reached into my pocket for chalk, yet the rhythm of my heart had other ideas, syncopating with the silent melody of this persistent crush.

I made a mark where the buttons strained slightly against the cloth, offering no commentary beyond the technical. "We'll lower these to provide a better line." I stuck a curved pin into the cloth.

"Is that what you're thinking about?" There was hint of mischief in her tone, a playful challenge in her voice as I focused on the suit's fit.

"Always," I assured her, my answer a mix of truth and deflection. "The line, the fit—it has to be perfect."

"Perfect." Rocky's head dipped, her gaze tracking the path of my hands with unsettling attentiveness.

"Indeed." My reply was curt, a self-imposed barrier against the warmth of her attention. I took a step back, needing the space to regain control. "It's all about the details."

"Of course," she agreed, her eyes never leaving mine.

Every touch of chalk against fabric felt like writing a secret message only she could read. Each stroke a word in a language of longing I wouldn't allow myself to speak aloud. My fingers moved with practiced ease, but inside, my emotions were raw edges and frayed threads, like this suit.

The jacket hung off Rocky's frame like an afterthought, the fabric bunching just above her hips as if unsure of its purpose. I reached out, fingertips brushing against the fabric, ready to tug it into submission. Another round pin, curved away from her body. "Apologies." I kept my voice low and steady.

A stray loc fell across Rocky's nape, dark and tempting. The impulse to sweep it aside was almost overpowering, but professionalism held my actions at bay. Barely. As I grazed the skin just below her hairline, a shiver cascaded down her spine, a silent communication that screamed louder than words ever could. Our gazes snagged, tangled in a moment neither of us had planned for.

"Are you...?" Her question trailed off, but the tension in the air demanded an answer I wasn't sure how to give.

"Better," I said, pulling back my hand with a careful detachment. My fingers twitched, remembering the warmth of her skin and the involuntary response it had elicited. Desire tugged at my belly, hot and dark.

I refocused on the task at hand, circling to inspect the suit's waistline, and lower. As I smoothed the inseam, my knuckles brushed accidentally against the inside of her thigh. The soft sigh that slipped from Rocky's lips might as well have been a siren call, stirring something deep within me that I couldn't quite drown.

"I'm sorry, I guess I'm not used to...this level of care." Rocky looked ahead at the mirror, her voice laced with a vulnerability that was as disarming as it was unexpected. Midnight black eyes. "People fussing over me." Something about her demeanor told me that it was unusual to see her this caught off-guard. It made me wonder how much of her vulnerability she masked with humor and bravado.

"Sometimes it feels like we're always the ones taking care of others, doesn't it?" I replied, my voice softening as I met her gaze. "But right now, it's your turn to be taken care of. You have nothing to feel sorry for."

"Something like that." Rocky nodded, as she looked down and away. "I...I really appreciate that."

I tucked the tremor I felt at her admission to busy myself with the fabric, feigning an interest in the seams that rivaled my interest in the woman standing before me.

"Thank you, Cal." Her gratitude was a simple melody in the complexity of our shared space.

"Of course," I managed to say, though what I meant was so much more. A mix of unsaid emotions caught in my throat.

The finality of the click as the button fastened into place marked the end of our session. Rocky's reflection in the mirror stood sharper, more defined than when she'd first strode into my shop, her suit poised to sculpt to her form like a second skin.

"Perfect," I said, stepping back, my voice a half whisper lost amidst the soft rustle of fabric and the distant hum of city life beyond the walls.

"Thanks to you," she replied, a smile playing on her lips as she lifted her arms, inspecting the fit.

I gathered my notes, the paper crackling loudly in the silence that had settled between us. Each scribble was a reminder to uphold the professional distance my craft demanded of me.

I watched as Rocky carefully adjusted the shawl lapels of her tuxedo jacket, her movements fluid and confident. The fabric clung to every curve of her body, accentuating her strength and grace.

She stepped down from the pedestal and went back to the changing area.

I found myself lingering in the space she had just occupied, caught between the heavy weight of what had transpired and the promise of what could be. I busied myself with fixing the pocket square of a jacket that didn't need fixing at all.

Rocky re-emerged, shrugging her scrubs back on.

"Let me walk you out," I offered, leading the way through the store floor that felt charged with an energy I dared not name.

"Appreciate it." Rocky's steps slowed. She looked like she wanted to say something. I held my breath.

At the doorway, she hesitated—a deliberate, weighted pause. Her shoulders, usually carried with a calm confidence, seemed to anchor themselves with newfound intent as our eyes met.

"Cal." Her voice trailed off into the silence that enveloped us.

"Rocky?" My heart was a drumbeat pounding in my ears. I almost pulled back at the last second, fearing she could hear it, too.

Her hand reached out, a slow and purposeful motion, fingertips grazing my cufflink before settling warm and firm against my wrist. The contact seared through the thin material of my shirt, a brand of intimacy that left my skin tingling long after she lifted her hand away.

I had never, ever swooned in 35 years of life. Not *once*. And here I was, *giddy*. With a pulsing beat in my pants.

"See you next time." She held my gaze just a second longer than necessary before backing out the door with that same confident stride.

"Next time," I echoed, my voice barely above a whisper, watching as she disappeared from view. The door clicked shut, sealing away the warmth of her presence and leaving me alone with the echo of our encounter.

I leaned against the wall, wind knocked out of me as I tried to reconcile the sudden rush of emotions swirling inside me. My legs wobbled to rubber. Utterly useless. The attraction was undeniable, a tangible thing that now hung in the air like the fine threads of silk from the spools in my shop. It was raw and real, and not just a figment of some secret, one-sided longing.

I didn't know how to feel about this. I didn't know how I *should* feel about this.

My thoughts were a whirlwind of fear and excitement.

I wanted her. *God dammit.*

Could I afford to explore this? Was the risk of giving in to these feelings worth the potential fallout?

I had always prided myself on being in control, on maintaining a certain decorum within these four walls that had become my sanctuary. But Rocky unraveled me by barely lifting a finger.

I took a pause, letting the cool, central-conditioned air fill my lungs and clear my head. For now, there were new patterns to draft and fabrics to order. The door rang out again, jolting me from the moment.

Right now, I had a job to do. I tugged at my tape, forcing a smile.

"Welcome to Duke's Tailor Shop. What can I help you with today?"

Orange and Blue

THE SUBWAY CAR'S RHYTHMIC lurch felt like a drumroll to my Saturday mission. I was on the hunt, fueled by the anticipation of victory that had me tapping my foot against the grimy floor. The doors slid open at my stop, and I emerged under the Barclay Center right into the cacophony of Atlantic Ave, where the scent of street vendor Halal trucks mingled with car exhaust.

"Excuse me," I murmured, sidestepping a tourist oblivious to the urgency in my stride. My heart beat in tandem with the staccato click of my kicks against the sidewalk as I wove through the crowd, threading my way toward the sneaker boutique that harbored my prize.

I pushed open the shop door, a bell chiming overhead. The walls were lined with clear shelves displaying kicks like precious jewels. My eyes darted from one pair to another—high tops, low cuts, vibrant colors, all vying for attention.

The boutique's air, thick with the musky scent of fresh leather and rubber, quickened my heart with anticipation. I moved towards the display, my gaze laser-focused on the holy grail of sneakers—the custom Ewings glinting under the spotlights like prized artifacts. The signature deep blue and orange beckoned to me even more in stark contrast with the deep yellow of the wall.

"Can I help you find something?" A salesperson approached, her voice slicing through my focus. Her nametag said 'Jennie'.

A familiar citrus scent drifted past, sending a tingle down my spine. Someone was wearing *that* cologne.

"Actually, Jennie, I was looking for these—" Every sense honed in on the prize. My steps quickened, a mixture of excitement and urgency propelling me forward. From the corner of my eye, a movement mirrored my own.

Our hands, driven by a shared desire, reached out in a synchronized dance that neither of us had choreographed.

The tips of our fingers brushed, and a jolt shot through me, as if we'd connected a circuit charged with more than just the hunt for rare sneakers. Her skin against mine was brief but electric, sparking a tension that hung heavy between us.

"Rocky?" I called out, a smile breaking across my face despite the surprise. She turned, her presence commanding, her style an effortless blend of crisp lines and casual flair.

"Cal? Hey! Didn't expect to see you here." Her dark eyes held a glint of amusement. "Never took you for a sneakerhead."

"I have my moments." I grinned, arms crossed as I appraised her current choice of kicks—a pair of pea-green, suede classics.

"Guess we're full of surprises." Her laugh was warm honey.

"Seems so." I chuckled, my nerves tingling at the proximity. My gaze drifted back to the shelves, scanning, searching.

"Ahem," Jennie interjected, unwittingly severing the current. She looked over her shoulder in panic towards the stockroom door. "These have been flying out the door today! This is actually the last pair we have. No restocks for a couple of months at least."

I drew back my hand as if burned. My heart thrummed against my ribcage, threatening to burst through.

"You have the nerve to have good taste, too." Rocky brushed the back of her head, suppressing a grin.

"Thanks." I shrugged, feeling suddenly self-conscious under her approving gaze. "They speak to me, you know?"

"Like a good suit?" she quipped, and I couldn't help but laugh.

"Exactly." My fingers twitched with the urge to reach out and touch the smooth leather, but I held back, not wanting to seem too eager. "Hey, it's why the suit you picked out...it's gonna look sharp."

"Only because you're the one tailoring it," she countered smoothly, and warmth bloomed in my chest at the compliment.

"Flattery will get you everywhere," I joked, though the sincerity in her tone resonated within me, stirring something that felt dangerously close to hope.

"Isn't that the point?" Rocky's smile was infectious, and I found myself smiling back, caught up in the ease of our conversation amidst the sanctuary of sneakers and shared interests.

"Maybe." I glanced away, feigning interest in a nearby display to hide the flush creeping up my neck. "But let's not get ahead of ourselves."

"Never." Damn, her laugh was music. "One step at a time, right?"

"Right," I echoed, my pulse quickening at the thought of what those steps might lead to if I dared to take them.

Jennie looked back and forth between us and cleared her throat. "Which one of you is the lucky one today?"

"Cal should get them," Rocky declared, her voice firm yet gentle, like a promise whispered into the night.

"Really, you don't have to—"

"You saw them first." She waved it away, stepping away from the display. "I owe you. It's all yours."

My chest swelled with a warmth that wasn't entirely due to the gratitude washing over me. It was a chivalrous act, one that spoke volumes of the character beneath the casual coolness Rocky wore as effortlessly as a tailored suit. A part of me wanted to argue, to say we could find a way to both walk out satisfied, but another, stronger part recognized the sincerity in her gesture.

"Thank you." The words feeling too small to encompass the swell of emotion. "It means a lot."

Jennie broke in. "Would you like to be notified about the next drop? I can make sure you're at the top of the list and make sure you get a coupon for your trouble."

Rocky turned to Jennie. "Now that's what's up. Sure!"

"Cool. Can I have your best phone number and email?" She whipped out a tablet.

As I watched Rocky talk to Jennie, the sneakers somehow seemed less significant. The real victory lay in the unspoken agreement hanging between us, a thread of connection spun from generosity and mutual respect. It was fragile, yes, but no less real.

The hum of the boutique's air conditioner mixed with the low murmur of weekend shoppers and music as I strolled slowly down the sneaker display. Rocky walked beside me, her presence a steady current. We walked along the rows of sneakers, pointing out ones with interesting features. Jennie headed toward the stock room.

"Look at this." Rocky held the heel of a turquoise, yellow and orange high top sneaker. A designer's emblem winked back, stitched onto the sneaker with meticulous care. "Pure artistry."

"Absolutely," I agreed, tracing the stitch. "But sometimes it's about the subtlety, you know? The logo shouldn't scream for attention; it should just... be."

"Like a whisper," Rocky nodded, tapping her chin thoughtfully. "Yeah, I get that. Makes the statement stronger when it's not trying too hard."

I chuckled, surprised by our easy rapport. "Exactly." We moved on to laces—flat versus round, patterned versus plain. Rocky preferred the flair of a mismatched pair of laces, for a unique pop of color. Each detail unraveled more about us than the fabric we discussed.

"I'm partial to the classic flat lace," I confessed, watching her reaction closely.

"Me too," she grinned, her eyes lighting up. "Gives a clean finish. Though I've seen some round waxed ones that weren't half bad."

"True, they can give a pair of kicks a certain... elegance."

"Exactly," she echoed my earlier sentiment, and the familiarity of it sent a warm shiver down my spine.

"Ma'am?" Jennie emerged from the storeroom, the box in her arms disrupting our bubble of shared interests.

"Please, call me Cal," I corrected her, offering a smile as she handed over my prize. I pulled out my card to pay for the sneakers and scribbled my signature onto her pad.

"Sure thing, Cal. Enjoy your new pair."

"Thanks. And don't forget to contact me when the restock comes in," Rocky chimed in, scribbling her number on the pad she offered.

"Will do, Ms. Beckford."

With the sneakers securely under my arm, I followed Rocky out of the store, the door chime bidding us farewell. The city greeted us with its racket of honking horns and chatter, the scent of roasting meat weaving through the noise. My stomach chimed in, reminding me that breakfast had been many hours ago. Oatmeal would *not* hold me until I got back home.

"Smells incredible, doesn't it?" Rocky breathed in deep, her gaze tracking the source to Calypso Sabor across the street. The Latin-Caribbean fusion joint never, ever missed.

"Definitely does." My mouth watered at the prospect of tender brisket or pasteles. I could almost taste the tang of barbecue sauce on my tongue, spicy and sweet in equal measure.

"Past lunchtime, huh?" She shrugged, though the glint in her eye suggested a shared understanding that we were both reluctant to part ways just yet.

"Yeah." My mouth watered as my eyes landed on the restaurant. "Way past."

The city's pulse thrummed beneath my feet as I shifted the sneaker box under my arm, contemplating the trek back to the quiet of my place. The thought was a cold splash against the warmth of Rocky's presence beside me. "I should probably head back," I ventured, though my voice lacked conviction.

"Hey." Rocky casually tilted her head towards the red-brick restaurant. A mural of a pretty Latina was spray painted next to the glass doors. "You hungry? We could grab a bite, just hang out for lunch. No big deal."

My breath hitched at the casual invitation, and I found myself caught in the steady gaze of her dark eyes. "I don't know if—"

"What, do you have somewhere else to be?" That smirk of hers was lethal. Should come with a warning label.

I saw an image of me, sitting alone at a laptop eating an oxtail platter from a Styrofoam container, doomscrolling social media while half-listening to *SVU* on television. Exciting. "No, but, uh. I guess spontaneity isn't exactly my strong suit." The corner of my mouth twitched upward despite the turmoil inside.

"Looks like today's full of firsts then." Rocky stepped off the curb with the confidence that seemed to be her second skin. She rubbed at her stomach. "I don't know about *you*, but I'm going to get me some jerk chicken."

I weighed my options. On one hand, I knew that once I finished work on Rocky's suit, we would probably never see each other again. Whatever connection this was would fade into the realm of missed opportunities. A missed jumper shot at the buzzer.

On the other hand, the allure of spending more time with her, even if it was just for one lunch, tugged at me.

Rocky's smile, shadowed briefly by a hint of something deeper, something I wanted to know, fueled my curiosity.

"Alright." I surprised even myself with the newfound boldness in my voice. "Let's do it. Lunch sounds perfect."

I followed. Good sense tucked away, my heart was a rhythm of possibility that played in my chest. As we approached the entrance to Calypso Sabor, I caught a glimpse of our reflection in the window—just two bros hanging out—and wondered if this was how it felt to blur lines meant to be crossed.

Just Two Bros

PUSHING OPEN THE DOOR to Calypso Sabor, a wall of warm air embraced us. The smoky sweetness hung heavy, awakening a hunger I hadn't realized was gnawing at me.

"Smells incredible." Rocky's eyes reflected the flicker of grill flames from the open kitchen.

"Doesn't it?" My stomach seconded the motion with an untimely growl. We shared a laugh, breaking the tension that had sprouted between us ever since the suggestion of this meal—this date?

"Smoked ribs sound good to you?" Rocky held the door open for me. It felt odd to have someone hold the door open for me for once. I was so used to hanging back, holding the door for others out of habit and courtesy.

"This is *so* not fair." The scent of charred wood and simmering sauces enveloped us like a welcome from an old friend. My stomach growled its approval again, determined to embarrass me in front of company.

Inside the restaurant, the atmosphere pulsed with energy. The walls, adorned with black and white aged photographs, whispered stories of the countless patrons who had passed through these doors. The worn-out dinette chairs and rickety tables held an air of nostalgia, as if they were witnesses to decades of laughter, conversations, and shared moments. Reggaeton music played from speakers high in the corner at the back of the restaurant.

People lined up at the takeout counter, their eyes fixed on the colorful menu boards, one half in the colors of the Jamaican flag, the other half in the red, white and blue of the Puerto Rican flag. The clatter of utensils against pans echoed in symphony with the lively chatter of diners. The scent of roasting meat hung thick in the air, weaving its way through the hubbub and nestling into my every sense. It was a scent that invoked memories of cookouts and lazy summer afternoons.

"Sounds like someone agrees with me." Rocky snickered, and I couldn't help but snicker along, finding her laughter infectious.

"Thanks for... you know, back there with the sneakers." The way my voice warbled was nails on a chalkboard annoying.

"Hey, it's nothing." Rocky shrugged, her ease soothing my lingering doubts.

"Still," I persisted, "it means a lot."

When we had both put in our orders, I instinctively pulled out my card, and Rocky dug into her pocket at the same time.

"Let me," I said, more firmly than I'd intended. I held up the bag with the sneakers. "It's the least I can do." My mind reeled with the memory of Rocky's hand yielding the shoe, her gesture both grand and intimate.

"Whoa there, Cal." Rocky laughed, her voice warm like the oxtail gravy that coated the rice we'd devour soon. She laid her own hand atop mine, halting me mid-reach. "What about splitting it? Going halfsies this time?"

Her proposal was light, teasing, but beneath those words danced the promise of something else, something that shot a thrill down to my fingertips. The implication of owing—of another meeting—left me momentarily breathless.

"This time, eh?" I tried to match her playful tone despite the pounding in my chest. My voice shook a little. "Is that your sly way of saying you want to do this again?" A nervous tick raced up my spine at the prospect of another date, and I tried to tamp it all the way down. This felt like playing with fire. Each word, a lit match tossed back and forth, the potential for ignition hanging between each syllable.

"Would that be so bad?" Rocky raised an eyebrow, a playful glint in her eyes.

The cashier looked between us with a smirk.

"Bad? No, not at all," I stammered. My cheeks burned with heat. Signing the receipt gave me only the tiniest bit of a shield from her, and the cashier, who was listening to every word. I managed a smile that I hoped looked more infectious than awkward. Caught off guard, I could only manage a shaky, "I, uh, just wasn't expecting that."

We walked back to the table, Sorrel drinks in hand.

Rocky shrugged. "How about this: I get a chance to properly wine and dine you later. I mean, I can't promise five-star dining, but I can definitely promise five-star company." Her hand retreated, leaving a tingling trail. Her words that hung in the air were casual, yet charged with possibility.

This was *not* two bros hanging out.

My mind raced as I tried to process Rocky's bold assertion. It swayed me, like a gust of wind on a summer day. The air around us seemed to shimmer, the bustling restaurant fading into the background as her words echoed with the pounding in my ears.

"Properly wine and dine me?" I repeated, blinking.

Rocky leaned forward, her dark eyes searching mine, concern etched across her brow for the first time. "Hey, did I overstep? I don't want you to feel pressured into anything here."

I glanced down, fiddling with the paper wrapper on my straw. "No, that's not it. I just..." I trailed off, unsure how to articulate the storm raging within me. Thoughts of my father's disapproving gaze flashed through my mind, and the weight of expectations pressed down.

"It's okay, take your time." Rocky reached across the table, her fingertips just barely grazing mine in a tentative show of support. My heart jack-hammered at the touch. God.

I let out a shaky breath, steadying myself before meeting her earnest eyes again. "I'm just...not used to this. Being pursued this way." I gestured between us. "By someone so much like...me."

Rocky tilted her head, brow furrowing slightly. "What do you mean?"

"I mean, two studs. Together." I gave a nervous chuckle. *Wow*, I was explaining this badly. "It's not exactly something I ever pictured for myself. My dad, he's pretty old school Caribbean. Very traditional."

"Ah, I got you. " Rocky nodded slowly, understanding dawning on her face. She leaned back in her chair, regarding me thoughtfully. I could see that she was being very intentional about her words. "So even though there's this, this attraction between us, taking that next step feels..."

Scary. Wild. Out of control. My body didn't listen to me anymore when she was even within sniffing distance. "Complicated." I tilted my head, fists balled up tight. "And risky. If word got out, it could jeopardize everything I've worked for with the shop."

"I got you. I know this type of connection is unexpected. Our chemistry...it goes against things we've been taught to expect." She clasped her palms as she spoke, regarding me openly but without pressure. "I just mean...maybe we don't have to force this into anyone else's rules. Maybe we get to feel this out in our own way."

Rocky gave me a small, reassuring smile. "No expectations, no pressure. Just putting that out there."

She leaned back a bit, allowing me space to process while still keeping that doorway open between us. Her energy remained open and calm, inviting without demanding. Non-judgmental. In her eyes, I saw patience, empathy, and something that looked remarkably like care. Probably the same care she showed her patients. She was likely used to holding a part of herself back to care for others. Or, to protect other people's feelings. Something loosened ever so slightly within my chest, seeing a mirror in her.

This wasn't about nameless, faceless people judging me or upholding some abstract reputation. This was about my father.

Shit. It had always been.

I unclenched my hands, my breath catching in my throat as the epiphany struck. World just rocked completely off-axis by that thought.

I lifted my eyes to Rocky's, seeing my own surprise reflected there. "I just realized...it's not even about anyone else. It's my dad. Apparently, I'm still afraid to disappoint him."

Like a sucker gut punch, saying the words out loud knocked the breath right out of me. I sat back in my chair. All this time I thought I was just doing what was necessary to protect the family business, when really, I was still that little girl in pigtails seeking my dad's approval.

"I get it, I really do." Rocky's gaze softened as her voice trailed off, a shadow of vulnerability in her eyes. I felt a tug in my chest, her words echoing my thoughts. "Wanting your father's approval is something that never truly goes away. Let's just say I'm grateful to have Unc in my corner." Our eyes met in a moment of silent understanding. We saw each other deeper than we knew.

I found myself leaning in, drawn by an invisible thread, my pulse echoing a rhythm of newfound connection. It was a subtle shift, almost imperceptible, but it felt as significant as any bold declaration.

For the first time, silence.

Rocky nodded slowly, her eyes never leaving mine. "I understand where you're coming from, Cal. And I would never want you to do anything that doesn't feel right or that could mess up your business. For obvious reasons. Jayla would flay me alive, for starters."

Even I had to laugh at that.

She absently stirred the ice in her cup with her straw. "But I also don't want you to think you have to hide how you feel, either. At least not around me."

With anyone else, this conversation would have shut down long, long ago, but her sincerity resonated through me. I wanted so much to let go and trust her. "I can do that."

Rocky seemed to waver, her usual confidence fading. She glanced down, fiddling with the edge of her napkin, hesitation playing across her features. When she met my eyes again, I glimpsed uncertainty there.

"Hey, why don't we...take things one day at a time?" Her suggestion came gently, almost nervously. "No pressure, we'll figure the rest out."

I smiled back, the tightness in my chest loosening. We didn't have to define this undefinable thing between us yet. Rocky wasn't pushing me away. She was willing to meet me at this thin line where I stood.

No one had ever done that for me before. Most women wanted to rush headfirst into something, often leaving me behind when I couldn't—wouldn't—follow. I've had a few subliminal social media posts directed at me in my lifetime from those women who felt slighted by my inaction. Relief whooshed out of me, but as I read the sincerity in her eyes, the weirdest, tiniest ember of disappointment sparked bright and hot. Is that what longing felt like?

Our food arrived then, the tangy aroma temporarily shifting our focus.

Rocky rubbed her hands together as she opened her container, and steam from the hot food rose out of it. "You may not ever look at me the same again after I lay hands on these ribs."

She might not look at me the same either after I demolished these jerk wings and alcapurrias. I swallowed a sip of my hibiscus ginger drink. "Listen, this is a judgement-free zone!"

As we finished up our meals, conversation flowed easily between us, from sports to books and everything in between. I found myself enthralled not just by her beauty, but by how our minds seemed to click, sparks igniting with each passionate opinion or quip.

She pointed a plastic fork at me, the tips stained with saffron yellow rice and peas. "You know, you're alright, even if you have horrible taste in football teams."

I dropped the paper napkin, feigning offense. "At least mine has won our division in the last decade, unlike some people's teams."

Too soon, though, our plates lay empty, and we couldn't put off the impending goodbye any longer. Outside the restaurant, an uncertain silence blanketed the space between us. There was so much unsaid, yet so much hope in Rocky's eyes as she gazed at me.

"Thanks for lunch," she finally said. "Gotta admit, I really enjoyed seeing you outside of the shop."

"Me too." I hoped she caught the double meaning as I smiled back softly. I liked far more than just talking fabrics and measurements with her. She understood the weight that unspoken things held, had since the day she walked through the shop door. And that scared me as much as it thrilled me.

She glanced down, an unusual shyness passing over her face as she tucked a loc behind her ear. "I should probably get going."

I nodded, whole heart a sinking anchor at the thought of her leaving. "Me too. Are we still on for Wednesday after next? Your last fitting?"

Rocky winked. "I'll wear my extra bright green jersey for you."

I rolled my eyes as I watched her gather the platter onto her tray. "Then I'll bring my sunglasses."

Rocky gave a playful laugh, her eyes sparkling with a mischievous glint. "Deal. And maybe, just maybe, I'll let you take me out to a game someday. Convert me to your team."

"See you later, Rocky."

Rocky stood there, her radiant smile fading slightly as she got up from the table. She hesitated, seeming to wrestle with her words. Her eyes held mine, two dark pools brimming with possibility. "I meant what I said, about seeing you again," she finally said, voice soft yet adamant. "Think on it?"

I gazed back. "I will," I managed, the promise feeling weighty on my tongue. We lingered in it a moment longer.

I could tell she was just as hesitant to leave as I was to see her go, but she took off with a nod. As she walked out of the restaurant, my eyes followed her. Rocky returned my look, just before she disappeared out of sight.

Callaloo

I REACHED OUT AND grabbed an oven mitt, twirling it playfully in my hand as the savory smells of spices and meats from my parents' kitchen wafted towards me. We had just put the roast into the oven. I hummed along to the new Marsha Ambrosius song as I grated the last bit of cheese for the macaroni pie into a large glass bowl.

Mama moved with a slow grace that was more cautious than her usual culinary ballet. Her knotty fingers fumbled over the bell peppers, their vibrant skins a stark contrast to her frustration.

"Here, let me help with that." I slid the knife from her grip. The blade sang against the wooden cutting board as I took over, my hands steady where hers were not. With each slice, the crisp snap of the bell peppers punctuated the rhythm of my thoughts—a staccato beat as I mulled over the events of the last week, the Saturday afternoon spent in Rocky's company. We had spoken every night since then.

My fingers did a quick solo on the knife's handle, drumming excitement and apprehension in equal measure. I wanted to tell Mama about Rocky, about the laughter and easy conversation that filled our time together. But fear clung to me, a persistent vine that threatened to choke out my courage.

"Lisha, you've been humming all morning," Mama's voice carried a note of curiosity. "You're like a teakettle on the brink of whistling. What's got you so chipper?"

"Ah, just had a good day out with a friend, that's all," I hedged, the words tumbling out before I could corral them.

"Is that right?" She peered at me, her eyes soft yet keen, seeing right through my half-hearted shield. My tongue felt thick with unsaid truths as I diced onions, their sharp scent mingling with my rising anxiety. But there was something about Mama's gaze, understanding and patient, that nudged the truth closer to the surface.

"Come on now, baby. You know you can talk to me." Mama's encouragement was gentle, a poke rather than a push. It made the space between us feel safer, even if the leap still seemed daunting.

"Alright, alright," I relented with a sigh, pausing to swipe at my eyes—onion-induced tears or otherwise, who could say? "I did spend the day with someone. Just didn't want to make a big deal out of it."

"Someone special, maybe?" A smile played at the corners of her lips, a mix of mischief and maternal pride that somehow always coaxed my guard down. "Well, I'm glad to hear it. It's high time my Calisha found someone worth her time."

"Mama, we're just friends." I blinked back a stinging tear, rubbing the back of my wrist against my eyes. Mama reached around me to turn on the water, an old trick that always worked. The water was supposed to draw the strong onion smell away from the eyes. Not this time, though.

Between the two of them, Mama had always been more accepting. She had seen and befriended too many people like me during her upbringing in Los Angeles to *not* be.

She wasn't done prodding me. "I never acted like that after spending time with a friend, except if he was a *gentleman* friend."

I set the chopped onion aside, scraping the diced bits into another glass bowl, and turned my attention to the squash.

The okra lay splayed across the cutting board, each slice a deliberate act by Mama's shaky hands. I watched her fingers work, plucking seeds with a slowness and care that seemed almost reverent. She glanced up at me, her eyes narrowing slightly—not in suspicion but with an intuition honed from years of motherhood.

Silence swelled between us, comfortable as an old quilt, as the garlic I had minced earlier began to perfume the room. It was a fragrance that spoke of countless meals shared, of laughter and sometimes tears, all within these walls that had borne witness to our family's history.

"Did I tell you about Charles Jenkins's oldest daughter?" Mama broke the silence, her voice threading through the garlicky air. She scooped scallions into a neat pile, her knife making a rhythmic sound against the wooden board. "She finally had the baby."

"It's about time. Last I heard, she was ready to write him an eviction notice. Forty weeks was enough!"

"Yep, and Charles went down to the hospital, suited up in one of your creations," she continued with pride swelling her chest. Her eyebrows held mischief. "Said he never felt prouder, standing there holding his first grandson, all thanks to his niece's new favorite tailor."

I hesitated, my heartbeat quickening as heat creeped up my face. The knife in my hand paused mid-chop, hovering over the squash that now resembled a wide checkered gradient of yellow and orange. "Mama!"

"Calisha Marie Duke." My full name. A rarity reserved for moments when she sought my full attention. Her eyes met mine, warm and filled with something like hope. "I told you I have eyes in the back of my head. Always have. Whoever this niece is, if she makes you happy, that's all that matters."

My throat tightened, warmth spreading from my chest to the tips of my ears. I set down the knife, the squash forgotten, and looked at Mama directly. "It's complicated," I admitted, though I knew she deserved more than my half-truths. I nodded towards the living room where dad sat.

Mama followed my gaze, her expression softening as she saw the distant figure of my father, lost in his own world of sports highlights blaring from the television. "Complicated, huh?" Mama repeated, her voice filled with understanding. "Well, you know your daddy, stubborn as a mule."

I reached for the pot, the steam warming my face as I swirled the wooden spoon through the simmering chicken. The collards and spinach tumbled from my hand, a cascade of leafy greens that dropped into the pot with a comforting hiss. Each stir blended the colors and scents, but it wasn't enough to keep my thoughts anchored to the task. They drifted, as they often did these past weeks, to Rocky.

"This woman must've really done a number on you. Your face is all lit up." The okra landed next to the squash on the cutting board, Mama's knife pausing mid-chop. Her eyes, always so perceptive, met mine with a glint of something new. Excitement, maybe? She slid the vegetables into the pot with care, and the coconut milk followed, a creamy swirl that promised richness.

"Her name is Rocky," I let the name slip out, watching the greens wilt in the heat. "We're just friends. But she's a...she's special."

"Is that so?" Her voice was light, teasing almost, and she tapped the edge of her spoon against the rim before setting it down. "Tell me about Rocky."

I leaned back against the counter, arms crossed over my chest as if they could shield this thing I was trying to protect. "She came in for a suit. For a wedding." The words were simple, but their weight pressed on me, heavy and undeniable. "She works at the hospital. A year older than me. Funny. Likes sneakers. Anime. Plays basketball. *Single* single."

"Ah." That smile of hers didn't falter, didn't judge. Instead, it spread wider, crinkling the corners of her dark eyes. "And this Rocky, does she make you happy?"

"Happy and terrified," I confessed, my hands unfolding to grip the edge of the counter behind me.

"Good. It's about time," she said, stirring the concoction that filled the kitchen with homely warmth. "You deserve love, Lisha. Just like anybody else."

"Even if it comes in unexpected ways?" I asked, the apprehension in my belly twisting tighter.

"Well, *especially* then." Her affirmation wrapped around me like one of the bespoke jackets I tailored, fitted and perfect.

"Thanks, Mama." My gratitude stretched beyond the callaloo or even the walls of the kitchen—it embraced the acceptance she offered without condition.

The lid of the pot clinked softly as I nestled it into place, sealing in the mingled scents of our labor. I watched Mama's back, straight and sure, as she made her way to the living room, where Dad sat with his newspaper, a thin barrier against the world he kept at a wary distance.

"Roland," Mama began, her voice carrying through the archway, both tender and insistent. "Lisha has something to tell us."

Did I? I held my breath, a plea for silence lodged in my throat, unspoken but fierce in its desperation. But Mama, bless her heart, was a jubilant tempest that could not be contained.

"Your daughter—" She paused, and I imagined her hands, those capable hands, resting on Dad's shoulders. "She's met someone special."

A chill rippled through me, despite the kitchen's warmth. I leaned on the countertop as my feet dragged towards the living room, knuckles whitening, as Dad's chair creaked—a herald of the storm about to break.

"Eh?" His tone sharpened, a knife edge of disapproval. After his stroke, the vowels weren't as crisp. "Who is he?"

Silence stretched, taut as a stitch pulled too tight.

Mama put her hand on her hip. "Roland, you know good and well that Lisha doesn't date boys."

Dad shifted around and looked me up and down, his gaze searching for answers he was not ready to accept. "Business is doing well, yes?"

"Yes, Dad." I stared out at the sunlit yard rather than meet his gaze. I was no more than patched suits on faceless mannequins under his impassive appraisal. "The shop is doing well these days."

His quick nod was the only flicker of pride he allowed me to see before his expression hardened again.

"You and your shop, Roland." Mama tossed a dishcloth onto her shoulder as she turned on her heel toward the kitchen. "If only you were as proud of your daughter as you are of that shop."

Dad sucked his teeth, muttering something I couldn't hear. The indistinct murmur of the television filled the silence. I made intense eye contact with the floor.

"Have you thought about whom to bring on in the shop? It's good to start them hands early while they're still limber."

I bristled. "You know it's been just me since..." I trailed off.

"What about bringing cousin Reggie on?"

His reference to my cousin landed heavily between us. I knew what he was implying, even if left unspoken—that Reggie could take over the shop someday if I didn't have...other plans. Children.

Dad tapped his fingers on the remote once. "Stroke took me early. Can't have that for you."

I shifted slightly, the unspoken expectations weighing heavy. "I'm careful about my health, Dad." I saw myself sitting at the table with Rocky, inhaling fried alcapurrias. "Mostly."

He grunted. His brows drew together, thoughts churning behind his eyes. "Shop should stay with family."

I pressed my lips thin, feeling the walls that kept me from ever truly being enough closing in. "It will," I replied quietly. "I'll...figure something out."

Dad sighed, his rigid posture softening ever so slightly. "Still time to sort the shop proper." He waved a resigned hand. This was clearly hard for him. "So, tell me...this friend. She treat you well?"

I blinked, surprised. His question caught me off guard after bracing myself against his disapproval. "I—yes, she's wonderful," I managed. "I really like her, Dad."

"Hm." He nodded, the closest thing to interest I'd heard yet.

I seized the opening, hesitant but hoping. "We met when she came in for a suit fitting."

I kept it brief and cautious, watching Dad's face. His eyes narrowed a fraction, but he nodded for me to continue. The details didn't matter. Just this chance to share this part of myself without shutting down was enough. There would be time later to work through the rest.

Behind us, things were suspiciously quiet. Not a single pot stirred or bowl clinked, just the slow bubble of a pot of callaloo. The shadow my Mama cast against the wall disappeared back into the kitchen.

A Particular Shade of Green

THE CHIME ABOVE THE door heralded her arrival, a burst of Seattle pride in the form of a bright green jersey. Rocky sauntered into my shop with that easy confidence that made the air seem lighter. I couldn't help but raise an eyebrow at the combination of Seahawks colors against the polished wood and fabric-filled interior of my tailor shop.

I rolled my eyes. "You've got to be kidding me."

"Now why would I miss this opportunity to show off my impeccably stylish uniform from *the* best team," she teased, a playful glint in her dark eyes as she pranced around.

"Stylish is quite the word for a Seahawks fan." I could not suppress the smirk tugging at the corner of my mouth. "Especially wearing that blinding shade of green."

Her laughter was a comfortable sound, wrapping around the room like an embrace. I turned away, hoping she didn't catch the flush creeping up my neck. My hands rubbed together quickly; today's fitting wasn't just any fitting—it was *the final* fitting.

"Ready to be wowed?" I asked, more to keep my hands from trembling than out of actual curiosity. I reached for the garment box that housed the result of weeks of meticulous labor.

"Always," she replied, her tone light but carrying an undercurrent of anticipation mirroring my own.

I opened the garment box deliberately, revealing the burgundy damask tuxedo that had occupied so many of my waking thoughts—and, if I were honest, a few dreams as well. The rich pattern seemed to come alive under the boutique's lights, waiting for Rocky to bring it its final form.

"Wow, Cal... this is something else," Rocky breathed out, stepping closer to inspect the craftsmanship. Her fingers hovered just above the fabric as though she could feel the hours of work through proximity alone.

"Made to measure." My hands brushed along the lapels, ensuring every stitch was in place before presenting it to her. "For you."

Her gaze lifted to mine, and I felt a flicker of something electric in the space between us. Was it her gratitude or my own hopefulness that charged the atmosphere?

"Let's get you into this suit, then," I suggested, steering clear of the intensity of that moment. Action was always safer than words. Words could betray too much.

"Can't wait to see how it looks," she said, her smile genuine, reassuring. But it didn't ease the ball of nerves in my gut. Because this suit wasn't just fabric and thread; it was a confession woven into every seam.

Rocky disappeared into the changing area, her silhouette merging with the soft glow of the dressing room lights.

Despite the composure I had crafted over the years as a tailor, this moment was always a lead weight in my stomach. There was always the tiniest room for error. A client who might not like a specific house detail, or had envisioned a different fit.

The rustle of fabric from behind the screen set my heart racing. It was just a suit fitting, something I'd done a hundred times before—me and Dad—but as Rocky stepped out, everything felt different. The tuxedo jacket hugged her broad shoulders like it had been made for them—which, of course, it had. But seeing it in reality? That was something else. The neat, creased pant was a perfect fit, with details matching the jacket.

"Allow me?" I offered, my voice steadier than I felt.

"Please," she said, turning slightly to give me access to the jacket.

My fingers trembled as they approached the silk lining, brushing against her back to straighten the fit. I could feel the heat radiating from her skin, even through the layers, and it made my head swim. My hands traveled to her front, making minute alterations, the proximity an excuse to memorize the curve of her collarbone—a detail so small yet so intimate.

I circled her, tugging at the hem, smoothing the shawl lapel. She watched me work, her gaze following every movement. "You're going to be the sharpest one there," I said, more to myself than to her, unable to stop a smile from forming at the thought. "That damask pattern is a classic—bold but not overbearing. Just like you."

"Thanks, Cal. It's perfect." Rocky blushed, her appreciation sending a wave of pride through me.

"Nothing but the best for my clients," I replied, trying to sound nonchalant while my heart did somersaults.

"Especially when your client is decked out in Seahawks colors, huh?" she quipped, lifting an eyebrow playfully. "Is it too late to change the detail to lime green?"

"Let's not get *too* carried away, now." I feigned disdain but failed miserably. Her laughter was a balm to the nerves I hadn't admitted were frayed.

"Your work really is amazing, Cal," she said after a moment, her tone softening. "Unc was right."

"Thank you." I ducked my head, feeling the need to hide my face. I wasn't used to praise, not like this, not from someone whose opinion suddenly meant more than it probably should.

"Seriously, you've got an eye for detail that's..." she trailed off, searching for the word.

"Obsessive?" I glanced up to catch the twinkle in her dark eyes.

"Passionate." Something about the way she said it made my belly tighten.

"Passionate," I echoed. I allowed myself the luxury of believing it, just for a second. "Turn around, Rocky." My voice held steady despite the swarm of butterflies in my stomach. She complied, and as she faced the mirror, the burgundy damask fabric of the tuxedo hugged her form made for her. It was made for by these hands that suddenly felt too clumsy to belong to a tailor.

"You really did the damn thing." Her eyes met mine in the reflection. "Cal, it's like you stitched swag right into the lining."

"Every single stitch," I confirmed, my gaze lingering on the way the suit accentuated the taper of her upper body down to the sleek lines of her waist and hips.

"Mind if I snap a picture for the website?" I asked, pulling my phone from my pocket. This was routine, something I'd done countless times before, but as I framed her in the camera's eye, everything felt different. Changed so much from when she first walked through the door.

"Sure thing." She posed with a playful wink, the corners of her mouth lifting in a smirk that could've been my undoing.

"Got it," I said, though I wasn't entirely sure my voice carried.

We moved over to the counter where the final bill lay between us—a paper barricade that seemed more substantial than it should have. She glanced at it, then back up at me, a mischievous glint in her eye.

"Perfect fit, perfect suit... just missing the perfect date," she teased, leaning ever so slightly across the counter.

Heat spread from my cheeks down to my neck. "Oh, any woman would be lucky to be your date," I fumbled with the receipt tray as I slid it across to her.

"Maybe," she drawled, signing her name with a flourish. "But there's only one woman who knows how to make me look this good."

Her words hung between us, a challenge and a confession all at once. My heart threatened to beat right out of my chest, pounding a rhythm that matched the racing thoughts in my head.

"Rocky, uh..." I started, suddenly stopping. What was I doing? This was new territory, uncharted and intimidating. But the hope in her eyes urged me on. "Maybe I should be the one thanking you." My voice rang barely above a whisper. "For trusting me with this, for making all the work worth it."

She reached out to squeeze my hand. "The pleasure's all mine."

My skin buzzed where she touched me, a jolt of electricity that sparked the possibility of something more. Something beyond tailor and client, beyond fittings and football rivalries. Something that felt like the start of a story I had never allowed myself to write.

"Thank you," was all I could say, but as our eyes locked, I knew she understood every unspoken word.

The silence stretched, a fine thread ready to snap. I studied her expression—eyes that seemed to pierce right through me, seeing parts of my soul I'd kept hidden under layers of fabric and stitches. The way her mouth quirked up.

"What are you thinking?" Her tone was gentle, coaxing. She turned from her reflection to face me.

For once, I wanted—no, needed—to be the one to take the leap, to meet her where *she* stood this time. I took a measured breath, releasing it slowly. My fingers grazed along the edge of the counter, seeking purchase in a world suddenly tilting on its axis. "Just picturing you at the wedding, is all." The words tumbled out, dusted with the quiet truth of my thoughts. "You'll be dancing under the stars, looking sharp enough to cut the night."

"Only if the stars are lucky," she winked, a playful smile teasing her lips. But her eyes stayed fixed on mine, earnest, waiting for more.

"Maybe they will be," I murmured. The image unfolded in my mind, as vivid as if it stood before us. A dance floor laid out in a tent among the vines, the twinkle of fairy lights above, and the two of us together, lost in the rhythm of a song meant just for us. "Would you like that? To dance under the stars with me?" I dared to let the question hang between us.

Rocky's gaze softened, her smile wide and bright. "I would. Very much so."

My heart fluttered like the wings of a caged bird against my ribs, desperate for release. It was now or never. "Then let's do it," I kept my voice steady despite the tremor I felt inside.

Her hand reached out, fingers brushing against mine, sending a shiver up my arm. "Is that your way of asking to be my plus one, Cal Duke?"

"Guess it is," I replied, feeling the corner of my mouth lift in a half-smile. She deserved someone who could be bold, step out on faith for her. We both did.

"Then I accept," Rocky stepped around the counter. Her presence enveloped me, a warmth that seeped into my very bones.

Our buoyant laughter filled the room, chased by the giddiness of what we were about to embark on. I closed the distance, and her arms found their way around me, strong yet tender. It felt like every fitting, every stitch had led us here—to this precipice of change.

"Can't believe I'm doing this." My face burned hot as I whispered against the shoulder of her jacket.

"Believe it," she whispered back, her breath a caress on my skin. This time, her fingers found my chin and tilted my face to hers.

And then, her lips met mine. A kiss that was a promise, a leap into the unknown. It was nothing like the stories I'd heard or the ones I'd told myself—it was better. It was ours.

In the intimacy of my shop, surrounded by bolts of fabric and the scent of fresh-pressed linen, I kissed Rocky Beckford. In that moment, it wasn't about the suits or the styles; it was about us finding each other amidst the threads and the remnants.

And as our lips parted, a newfound sense of anticipation hung in the air like the delicate fabric swaying from the racks.

On The Vine

THE EVENING AIR WAS crisp, laced with the scent of fall as it swept through the vineyard. I nodded at Jayla, her wedding gown shimmering under the reception's fairy lights. "Congratulations," I offered, my voice threading through the laughter and the DJ playing Stevie Wonder's "As." She squeezed my hand. "Jaleel's a lucky man."

"Thanks, Cal." Jayla beamed, a picture of blissful matrimony. Her eyes flicked between Rocky and me, a mischievous glint sparking in them. "I saw the way you two clicked at the fitting. Who would've thought the tailor would snag the most eligible bachelor at my wedding?"

Rocky chuckled, hands rubbing the back of her neck. "Guilty as charged."

"Happy to see you smiling more these days, Rock." Jayla's gaze softened before she kissed us both on the cheek and shooed us away with a wink. "Thank you both for coming! Now go, enjoy the night."

We drifted from the tent, our footsteps crunching over gravel. Silence settled between us, comfortable yet thick with unspoken words, as we approached the hotel suite. The ambient light from the wedding tent cast a warm glow on the vine leaves.

"Nice place, huh?" Rocky's dark eyes reflected the starlight as if holding a secret conversation with the universe.

"Very," I agreed, watching the waning tent lighting play off her tuxedo pattern.

Once inside, I hung my jacket up with care, smoothing out the lapel. Rocky did the same, her movements fluid, unhurried. The room breathed with a pulse that seemed to push us closer together, inch by tantalizing inch.

"Goodnight, Cal." Rocky stepped forward, her voice a low thrum that vibrated through the space between us.

"Night." My reply was barely audible, even to my own ears.

Her lips met mine in a casual brush, a goodnight kiss meant to be quick, simple. But simplicity shattered like glass under the weight of suppressed longing. We lingered, the kiss deepening, hands tentatively exploring, mapping out territories long denied. Rocky's firm hands gripped my waist, fingers curling in desperation as she groaned into my mouth.

Was it too soon for this? How did two studs have sex with each other, anyway?

Our bodies gravitated towards each other in spite of that thought, the boundaries between friendship and desire blurring with each stolen touch. The current that ripped through me, pulsing in time with the steady thrum of Rocky's heartbeat. It drowned out the doubts and questions that had plagued my thoughts.

Then, as though waking from a dream, we parted, the sudden absence of her warmth leaving me adrift. "I—uh, goodnight," I stammered, retreating into my own room, the door clicking shut behind me.

Alone, my thoughts spun, weaving images of water cascading over Rocky's brown skin in the shower, droplets tracing paths I yearned to follow. I paced, the lush carpet swallowing the sound of my restless steps. My hands, so skilled with needle and thread, now clenched with the urge to stitch together every moment leading up to this one.

In the quiet of the hotel suite, I could almost hear the echo of our kiss, feel the ghost of her touch still lingering on my lips. My belly ached with desire. I leaned against the door, the wood cool against my forehead, and closed my eyes. The night whispered promises through the crack beneath the door. Would I be able to rest my head onto the pillow tonight unless I answered them?

The sound of Rocky's shower ceased, plunging the suite into a silence that seemed to pulse with the beat of my own heart. I sat on the edge of the bed, fingers laced so tight it hurt. My mind waged war. Courage scrapped with fear in the trenches of desire. Each drop of water that had whispered down her skin replayed in my head, tempting me to cross lines drawn by decades of practiced restraint.

I paced to the window. The vineyard outside sprawled like a promise under the moonlight, rows upon rows of vines standing testament to growth from the most intimate embrace of earth and sky. I wanted that kind of entwined existence, a connection to roots and reaching out.

I stopped, caught my reflection in the glass. I was a woman usually so certain with her hands, now uncertain of where to place them. I took a breath, released it, and the decision formed like a stitch pulled taut—I couldn't hold back any longer.

My steps to her door were both too slow and too fast. I knocked before my courage could unravel, the sound sharp in the quiet hallway.

Rocky swung the door open, the white robe she wore teasing with its loose tie. "Can't sleep?" Her voice was playful, but her eyes searched mine, keen as if sensing the shift within me.

"Something like that." Heart racing, I moved closer, until we were toe-to-toe.

She stepped aside, an unspoken invitation, and I entered the warmth of her room. It smelt of her, of steam and soap and something that was undeniably Rocky. Our space closed in heartbeat increments until I bridged it with a kiss that held all the silent conversations we'd ever shared.

Her response was immediate, a hand at the small of my back pulling me closer, her other tangling in the short strands of my hair. We moved with an urgency born of nights spent imagining just this. The kiss deepened, our breaths mingling, hands roaming.

"Cal," she breathed against my lips, a question and an answer all at once.

"Rocky," I returned, pressing our bodies close together. Our hands worked in tandem, peeling away layers as though unwrapping long-awaited gifts. I grasped Rocky's robe's belt and slowly pulled it open, revealing soft skin underneath. My fingers teased her sleeve tattoo. Teeth chattering against teeth, lips parting slightly, we kissed more fervently as Rocky's scent wafted towards me, mingled with the smell of her desire. Intoxicating. The robe fell to the floor, forgotten, and soon we stood there, bared souls reflected in bared bodies.

"Tell me what you want." Rocky's voice was a whisper, her hands poised at my hips, her gaze holding mine.

I nipped at her lips. "You. Just you."

She lifted a hand to lift my face to hers. "Teach me how to please you. I'll do the same."

"Touch me here," I guided one of her hands to my chest, right over my racing heart. "Feel what you do to me." The other, I guided towards my nipple, puckered with the need for attention, of a warm mouth. My mind flashed white-hot images of what I wanted. Me, underneath her grinding hips, ankles on her broad shoulders, her buried so deep we felt like one. Her tugging on my hips to ride her face as her tongue teased my folds. Something I had always wanted, but never had the courage to ask for with other lovers, until now.

Too soon? Not soon enough.

"God, Cal." Her touch was reverent, exploring with a tenderness that coaxed sighs from my lips.

"More," I urged, leading her to discover the landscape of my desire. My fingers danced along her sides, feeling muscular contours and still-damp flesh. "Need you inside."

Rocky gasped, eyes completely black. "Bed. Now."

We fell back onto the bed together, tangled like the vines outside the window, searching for each other's skin to taste and claim.

Rocky pulled away to nod towards her overnight bag. She looked shy, almost. "Don't judge me, but. I brought something."

I laughed, more than a lot turned on at the idea of taking her deep to the hilt. My thighs squeezed together, my walls clenched with desire. "A little hopeful?"

Rocky buried her head in my neck and groaned. "Just a little. Okay, a *lot*." She lifted her head to meet my gaze. "We don't have to use it if you don't want, my fingers and mouth work just fine."

"Mmm, and I want your mouth and fingers." My leg slid up the side of her muscular body, taking a wicked satisfaction as her body shuddered in response. "But I want that, too."

She jumped out of bed. "Say less."

Naked as the day she was born, she rooted around in her bag until she found the harness.

Grabbing the harness, Rocky's fingers trembled slightly as she fumbled with the buckles and straps until they were flush with her skin. The toy bounced heavily between her legs. Once it was secure on her hips, she crawled back onto the bed, a serpent gliding over sheets and skin. She hovered over me, her eyes flashing with hunger as she watched me watch her, naked and beautiful. I pushed her gently to the side. "Let me see you."

My mouth watered at the sight of her body, every inch of it calling to mine. Without thought, I leaned up and took one of her perfect breasts into my mouth, tongue swirling around the dark nipple before trailing kisses down her stomach, tasting the saltiness of sweat mixed with want.

Long, dark, thick locs hung loose around her shoulders and breasts.

"Beautiful," I murmured into her skin, never breaking eye contact. The heady, musky scent of her made me want to tug the harness off her to bury my face in her mound, fill my mouth with her. My clit throbbed, insistent.

Her hands dug into my hair, holding me close as she arched her back into me. "Fuck," she panted between gasps for air. "Mmm, Cal."

I rubbed my cheek against the toy. "Can I?"

Rocky's stomach quaked with laughter. "It's always the quiet ones, isn't it? God, yes."

I licked a stripe up the dildo, swirling around the tip with my tongue, looking her dead in the eye the whole time. Not everyone was into this, but by her pained expression, her ragged breaths and the way she tried desperately not to thrust into my mouth, she was. She *so* was.

My fingers trailed feather light circles around the insides of her thighs as I took it into my mouth, far as it would go. The other hand, I slid between my legs.

She zoomed in on my fingers, rubbing at my slickness, eyes at half-mast, delicious mouth parted. She sighed. "Wanna taste you."

I gave the toy one last lick and sat up, swinging one leg around her waist. The toy teased my slit. With one smooth movement, I removed my fingers from my slick mound and teased the entrance of Rocky's lips until she opened her mouth. She pulled my fingers deeper into her mouth, tongue and lips sucking eagerly.

She moaned like a woman starved.

Perhaps she was.

My other hand guided myself onto the toy, sinking slowly, carefully over her length. She watched with glazed eyes as I took it inside.

The pleasure of having her sink so fully inside me made my toes curl. "Rocky," I whined.

Rocky hissed in response, free hand clutching at the sheets and holding on for dear life. Each movement from either of us increased the pull, tugging at our skin, wanting more friction. "That's it," she panted, thrusting up to meet my downward strokes.

She whispered against my lips. "Come closer." I obliged, moving my body flush against hers and took her deeper inside me with each upward motion of her hips. We were mouth-to-mouth, nipple-to-nipple, mound-to-mound. The bed groaned under our combined heat and need as we found a rhythm that sent shivers up our spines. I ground my hips harder and faster against her, feeling her breath hitch with each thrust. The harness was hitting her just right, hitting us both just right. My thighs trembled with effort as every thrust pushed me closer to orgasm. There was only Rocky underneath me, her hands gripping my hips holding me up. Her eyes locked on mine.

We both got closer to the edge, the tip of my tongue tracing every fold and crevice of hers as we humped each other, sharing sweat and our combined juices. Skin slapped against skin. Heavy breathing and the bed creaking beneath us were the only sounds in the room.

Perfect.

Breathless cries echoed off the walls as we reached our peaks together, buckling under each other. Rocky's scent filled my nose with every unrestrained breath. I pressed my damp forehead against hers, kissing her gasping mouth until she froze, whimpering with the force of her climax. I tumbled over soon after, rocking hips jerking to a halt until I moaned into her mouth, clinging to her.

Waves of pleasure crashed over us like ocean waves upon shore; it was sweet release and heady satisfaction wrapped into one moment that seemed to last an eternity. I felt her soft lips on my neck, nipping gently at the pulse, still racing from our shared passion and I shuddered. I sat up to pull the toy out, hearing it release with a soft pop.

Round two, as tempting as it sounded, would have to wait.

We continued kissing each other until the shakes stopped, coming down off our high.

She spoke first. "Well, goddamn."

I snorted. "I know."

"No regrets?" Rocky murmured, trailing her fingers down my arm.

I nestled closer, a contentment sinking bone-deep. "Never."

As our bodies cooled, and the wild vigor of our lovemaking settled, a tender peace settled between us.

Rocky ran her fingers through my sweaty hair, her breaths slow and steady against my neck. I took her hand and kissed each knuckle in turn.

Soon enough, her breathing slowed even more. She wrapped an arm around my waist. I relaxed into her, feeling protected and warm. Finally safe enough to lay down my armor and show her the softness underneath my suits.

As I drifted off, I realized the truth I had resisted: another woman like me could be home.

***

Thank you so much for reading Bespoke! If you enjoyed this story, would you mind leaving a review?

THE END

About the Author

L.M. Bennett writes good stories about bad girls. (And good girls, too!)

She lives in northern Virginia with her fiancée. They are owned by a house panther and a house lion who can do no wrong in their eyes, but test them anyway. She enjoys sports, The Great British Baking Show, Jeff Goldblum and the holy trinity of coffee, wine and tacos.

Also By L.M. Bennett

Other Series

Competing Desires is the Las Vegas-based trilogy of love and rivalry in the worlds of Championship Poker, Mixed Martial Arts and Racing. High angst, action-packed, firecracker slow burn sports romances. Titles in the series include:

Bad Beat

Pit Stop

TAP OUT

Love Cynics Anonymous is a series of loosely-interconnected stories about young women who are avoiding love, but find it anyway. Some even manage not to mess it up. Sweet and spicy, slow burn romances. Other titles in the series include:

Corked!: An Enemies-to-Lovers Short (no spice)

Lesbian Speed Dating: A Short Story (no spice)

(re)twist – A [Hendrix/Fatima] Short Story

Bespoke: A Novella

String Theory: A Valentine's Day Novelette (no spice)

Crushed: A Novelette

You Were Almost Home

The Beats Between Us is an upcoming series about love, hip hop and authenticity set in Los Angeles. Titles in the series include:

The Art of Going Rogue

Kissing The Opps (Patreon Exclusive)

Christmas Curveballs is what it looks when it's Christmas and you're totally over it, but you meet your person because the universe has jokes. Titles in the series include:

The Cynic's Christmas Conundrum

The Connoisseur's Christmas Courtship (McKenna's Story)

The Chef's Christmas Charade